A Different Drummer

Thoreau and Will's Independence Day

by
Claiborne Dawes

Illustrated by
J. Stephen Moyle

Discovery Enterprises, Ltd.
Carlisle, Massachusetts

© Claiborne Dawes, Concord, MA 1998

ISBN 1-57960-039-5 paperback edition

Library of Congress Catalog Card Number 97-78303

10 9 8 7 6 5 4 3 2 1

Printed in the United States of America

Subject Reference Guide

A Different Drummer
Thoreau and Will's Independence Day

Written by Claiborne Dawes and illustrated by J. Stephen Moyle

Henry David Thoreau — Juvenile Biography

Walden Pond — Juvenile Historical Fiction

Summary

Young Will Crawford helps Thoreau move to his cabin at Walden Pond and learns another meaning for "Independence Day."

Acknowledgment

With special thanks to

Tom Blanding, Thoreau scholar and superior fact-checker

and to

The Concord Free Public Library

The Concord Museum

Bill Kenney

Kevin Mara

and Bill Dawes, who always knew it would happen.

Chapter One

The glorious Fourth of July began terribly . . . What I'd done wasn't so awful. Anyway, not bad enough to make me miss the town's parade. But Father said a ten-year-old boy should be smart enough not to carve his initials in Squire Hoar's favorite beech tree.

So he took away my jack-knife and forbade me to go to the Concord parade, and that's why I was sitting on our front steps with Jessie when Mr. Thoreau went by.

I'd heard the third signal gun, so I knew the procession was stepping out: the military escort, the Revolutionary soldiers, and the Boston Young Men's Whig Club, all carrying banners. They'd march to the Battle Ground, where we fought the British on April 19th 1775, seventy years ago. After some long speeches, they'd march to the depot, with my friends running behind. And I was missing all of it.

It was going to be a hot day. The sky was white, not blue, and the sun a white ball just topping the First Parish Church steeple.

"Don't you like parades, Will Crawford?"

A hay-wagon, with Mr. Hosmer's gray horses, had pulled up in the road, and driving it was Mr. Thoreau.

Mother hadn't said I had to stay on the porch. Anyway, she was practicing hymns on our seraphine in the parlor. So I got up and walked down to the gate with Jessie. She's our hound, mostly white with some brown here and there.

Mr. Thoreau looked down at me from the wagon. He was wearing a straw hat, and I could see sunshine through two small tears in the brim.

"Don't you enjoy parades?" he asked again. "Or are you ill?"

"No sir. Yes, sir, I like them a lot. But I cut my initials — well, two of them — in Squire Hoar's old beech tree yesterday, with my new knife, and Father said I couldn't go to the parade…or to the fireworks tonight in Boston, either."

"I'm very sorry to hear that."

Mr. Thoreau was a teacher in town. At least he had been. He and his brother, Mr. John Thoreau, had a private school for a while in the Concord Academy. Before that, he taught in the Center School, but the town school committee told him he wasn't strict enough. So he feruled some boys, including my oldest brother, Robert — hit them on their palms with a ruler. Then he resigned.

Father said Robert likely deserved it, if only for something he'd done and hadn't gotten caught at.

After that, my friends and I often met Mr. Thoreau walking in the woods. One hot day we saw him wading chest-deep in the Assabet River, wearing just his shirt and his hat.

The near horse stamped at a fly, making his harness jingle. "Brownie is anxious to be off," said Mr. Thoreau. "Almost as eager as I."

"Where are you going, sir?" I asked.

"I'm changing my abode," he answered.

I guess I looked puzzled. "I'm moving, young Will," he explained. "I've built a house by Walden Pond, and I intend to live there." He smiled and added, "Yes. Live, deliberately."

Walden Pond was a pretty little lake less than two miles from Concord center; even less, if we disobeyed our parents by walking there along the new Fitchburg Railroad tracks.

The off horse shook himself, and Mr. Thoreau climbed into the back of the hay-rigging to tighten some ropes. He had a table there, a desk, some chairs, a caned bed. There was a box or two of cooking things, some fire tongs, and a pair of andirons.

My brothers and I camped out sometimes, in a lean-to we'd built by the Concord River; but all we took were blankets and an old fry pan or two. This was different.

Brownie turned his head and blew into my hair. I rubbed his nose, then asked, "How long will you stay there?" I nearly forgot to add, "sir."

"I don't know," he answered, jumping down and coming over to the gate. "A year, perhaps. Or two."

A year.

A whole year. Two years.

I could hardly imagine it. To live by the pond, all day. Fishing. And skating. No church, no school.

"Who's going with you? Are you...?"

Mr. Thoreau was smiling. "I think the next question belongs to me," he said. "Would your father permit you to accompany me to the pond today? As you see, I have much to unload. We might have a swim, when we have finished."

Ride to the pond, behind Brownie and Bess. Spend the day there. Swim. It might be a glorious Fourth after all.

I knew what Father would say. He'd probably add something about the time Mr. Thoreau set some woods on fire, by accident, the year before.

Father said Mr. Thoreau spent too much time dilly-dallying around in the woods, that it was time he settled to some real work. He let us go berry-picking with Mr. Thoreau, or fishing, and he went with us — but only because Mother insisted — to the Thoreaus' melon party every summer. Mr. Thoreau grew the best melons of anybody.

"Father is at the parade, sir." I said. "With my little brother." Ben had waggled his tongue at me behind Father's back as they passed through the gate; he'd find a grass-snake in his bed that night. "But Mother is at home."

Mother was friendly with Mr. Thoreau's family, and she'd taken piano lessons from his sister, Miss Helen.

Mr. Thoreau took off his hat and smoothed his brown hair. I followed close behind him up the steps.

"You are up and about early, Mr. Thoreau," Mother said, when she came to the door.

"I find it unwise to keep my head too long at a level with my feet, ma'am," he said. After he'd explained the plan, he added, "I understand that young Will is being punished for a transgression. I am not offering him a holiday."

Mother hesitated. "Mr. Crawford and Robert are going to the fireworks in Boston. Will should be home when they return."

"I can promise that," said Mr. Thoreau. "We will have done a hard day's work."

I noticed he didn't mention swimming.

Chapter Two

"Keep your hat on, Will. The sun's very hot."
Mother's voice followed us as the horses
turned onto the Walden Road.
Mr. Thoreau kept the team at an easy walk; their big feet
stirred up puffs of white dust. The edges of the road were
lined with white cow parsley and yellow St. John's wort.
A hawk circled overhead, screaming its thin cry.

I looked up at Mr. Thoreau. From the side, you noticed
his long, hooked nose. When he felt me watching him, he
turned and smiled. His eyes were a greyish sort of blue.

All of a sudden, he pulled the horses to a halt, wrapped
the reins around the brake, and jumped down, motioning
to me to join him. Crouching beside the roadside ditch, he
pointed. Something moved in the shallow water: a turtle,
a big one, with a bright yellow throat and yellow spots on
its black shell.

"A Blanding's turtle," said Mr. Thoreau. "Rare hereabouts. I've seen but two others. Is it not beautiful, Will?"

Every rock in the Concord River held a couple of turtles, dozing in the sun, plopping off if a boat came too close. "Yes, sir. I guess so," I said.

"A female, I believe," he said. "Let us look for her eggs." Springing up, he jumped the ditch and began to hunt along the sandy bank.

I saw them first, nearly buried in wet sand.

"Sharp eyes, Will! Good boy." Together, we scraped away the sand and uncovered eight soft, white eggs.

"I would expect the Blanding's to lay in mud, a more saponaceous medium," he said thoughtfully.

"Sir?"

"Saponaceous: slippery. The root word is Latin, sapon, meaning soap." I'd never thought of words having roots.

We covered the eggs and were getting into the wagon when I heard a familiar bark. In the road behind us, panting and smiling, stood Jessie.

"Is she yours?" asked Mr. Thoreau.

"Yes, sir. I guess she followed us." Would we have to take her back?

"We shouldn't discourage such friendship. But you

13

must not let her chase the squirrels or chipmunks. They have come to trust me."

We climbed Brister's Hill, slowly. Soon after, Mr. Thoreau turned the team off the road. The wagon crossed a briar field and pulled up near a small, unshingled cabin on a hill among sumach and hickories. There was a woodshed, and a privy out back. Down a little slope, Walden Pond glittered in the sunshine.

Mr. Thoreau tied up the team and lifted a box from the back. "The sooner we have unloaded, the sooner we can swim," he called over his shoulder.

He was standing in the center of the cabin when I came in with an andiron under each arm.

"Welcome, Will!" he said. "You are my first real guest."

The cabin was one room, about ten feet wide and fifteen feet long, with two windows, both wide open; as we stood there, a chickadee swooped in one side and out the other. There was a garret, with a ladder going up to it. A trap door opened into a dirt cellar. The walls were unplastered; many of the boards still had their bark on them. The room smelled of fresh pine.

I wished it was me that was moving in.

"Now. Where shall we put the bed?" asked Mr. Thoreau.

I set down the andirons (there was no chimney or fire-place yet, just a stone foundation for them) and pointed to the western window. "Over there? You can see the pond."

"First thing in the morning. Excellent. As I told your mother, I rise early."

There was a sharp bark, then a scuffling and a squeak and the rattle of an angry squirrel from a nearby pine tree. "I dislike seeing any creature restrained, but I fear you must tie Jessie up," said Mr. Thoreau. "You'll find some rope in one of the boxes."

I tied her in the shade of some scrub maples, then brought the box indoors. Mr. Thoreau looked puzzled; then he laughed. "My sister Sophia has stocked my larder, despite my protests. She fears for my health here, though I tell her wildness is the best tonic."

The only tonic I knew was Connell's Balsam. Mother gave it to us every spring; being at Walden Pond was lots better than that.

"Miss Sophia's sent plenty of good things," I told him, lifting out a glass jar. "Applesauce, and two kinds of pickles, and grape jelly, and three loaves of bread." It was past my dinner time.

Mr. Thoreau wasn't ready to stop. We brought in the bed — just caning nailed to a low platform — and the desk, like a schoolmaster's with a hinged, sloping top, and a table, and three chairs. The smallest one had rockers, though no arms.

"I guess you won't be having many guests," I said.

"Three chairs will be enough, don't you think?" he asked. "One for when I'm alone. Two, for friendship. And three, at most, for...society."

16

I pictured our crowded parlor at home, with a dozen of Mother's sewing circle ladies, all chatting at once.

"Do you know why I have come here, Will?" He was leaning against the doorframe, his back to me.

I went and stood beside him. Sunlight dappled the pine needles at his doorstep. Walden lay cool and green through the trees. A chewink called, "Drink your tea—ea—ea," beyond the cove.

"I guess not, sir. Not exactly," I answered.

"To simplify my life. To make do with as little as I can. Things — our possessions — can own us, weigh us down. I crave freedom from belongings, Will. Is that not what today is about? Perhaps July 4, 1845 is my particular Independence Day."

With that, he took off his hat, hung it on a nail just inside the door, and said, "I need to start a fire on the beach, to cook our lunch. Then it will be time for a swim."

Jessie stood up and whined.

"Please, Mr. Thoreau," I said. "Can she come? I'll watch her."

"Why not? This is a holiday for Jessie, too."

Chapter Three

M r. Thoreau was a strong swimmer. After a while, he told me to stay in the cove — and to keep one eye on the cook fire. Then he struck out toward the deep green water in the middle of the pond.

There were tadpoles in the shallows. I tried collecting some in a jar, but Jessie kept biting at them, scaring them off, so I picked up a stick to throw for her. Stuck to it was a bunch of clear, jelly-like stuff.

I looked closer; inside the jelly there were lots of little roundish things.

"What have you found?"

Mr. Thoreau was standing at the edge of the water, rubbing himself dry with his shirt.

"I don't know, sir." I showed him the stick. "Some kind of eggs?"

"Excellent! Your tadpoles hatched from ones like that. A good-sized egg mass, Will. I must sketch it." And off he went, running toward the cabin.

Crouched in the dirt, he made several quick pencil drawings, while I turned the stick so he could see the whole mass.

"Why do you think the frog attached its eggs to that stick?" he asked as he worked.

"So they wouldn't float away?"

"That would be my guess. Frogs are amphibians, as you know, living on land and in the water: from the Greek words, *amphi bios*, double life. The young must hatch in water, but close to land. Nature arranges these matters very cleverly."

"Do you think Nature is like a person, sir?" I asked.

He was quiet for a bit, then answered, "I suppose I do. A teacher, in whose classroom we are all equal students. But I suggest you not mention that to the Reverend Frost." He grinned. "Do you know why the fish named pouts are also called preachers?"

"No, sir."

"Because they often give a squeaking noise when taken from the water."

I sure wasn't going to tell Reverend Frost that.

"Now, Will," said Mr. Thoreau, standing and brushing himself off, "I see our fire has turned to coals. I will try to catch a fish or two for our dinner. Perhaps you would pick us some peas. The patch is west of my bean field."

I'd have preferred fishing to picking peas, but I didn't say so.

You couldn't miss his bean field: miles of beans, it seemed. A lot of hoeing. Corn, too, and young potato plants. And turnips. Myself, I don't find those worth the trouble of digging.

With Jessie at my heels, I moseyed along in the warm dirt, picking pea pods, splitting a few open to get the tender peas inside. I was really hungry. I reached the end of a row, turned down the next, and hit my bare toe on something sharp.

It was an Indian arrowhead, a small white one, its edges chipped away to a fine point: the first I'd ever found by myself. Robert had half a dozen, but he wasn't about to trade me one, not even for my best fish hook. I put it carefully in my pocket.

Mr. Thoreau had caught a good-sized fish and was roasting it in wet paper over the hot stones. The smell made

my mouth water. We shelled the peas and sat down
on a log to wait while they boiled.

I handed him my arrowhead.

"A beautiful one, Will," he said, turning it over in his long
brown fingers. "I've turned up many in my bean
field, but none nicer than this."

"That's a heap of beans, sir," I said, returning it to my pocket.

"Too many for one? I do plan to sell some, and my
friend the woodchuck helps himself to supper there.
Ah, I believe the fish is ready."

He removed it from the fire and laid it on a flat rock.
"You do the honors, Will," he said, handing me his pocket
knife. "I know I can trust you with this, despite your
earlier error in judgement."

My face went hot, but I took the knife, unwrapped the
fish, and boned it carefully.

With the fish and peas we had bread that Mr. Thoreau
had baked the day before. It had that woody taste you get
from cooking over pine kindling.

When we'd eaten every scrap, Mr. Thoreau stretched
out comfortably, his head propped on one hand. "Do you
know, I committed a much greater breach of the law than
your attack on the squire's beech tree," he said. "But no
one punished me, except my neighbors, by their silent

disapproval."

"You mean the fire?" I said.

"Yes, the infamous fire, last year. Did you see it?"

"No, sir. We smelled the smoke, but Father wouldn't let us go with him to put it out."

"Just as well. It moved swiftly and caused much damage to the woods about Fair Haven. Edward Hoar and I were careless to light a cooking fire in such dry weather."

"You mean Mr. Edward?" I asked.

"Yes, the squire's son. Foolishness is not limited to ten-year-old boys, Will. Come," he added, jumping up. "let us finish our task. I want to take you boating before you go home."

We put out the fire and scrubbed our dishes with sand on the beach. He only had three plates, two knives, and a couple of forks, one cup, and one spoon.

We brought in the rest of his boxes, two of them full of books. There was an instrument too — a flute — wrapped in a piece of flannel.

Mr. Thoreau took it gently from me. "My brother John's," was all he said. Then I remembered. Mr. John had died, a couple of years before. I didn't know what to say, so I started to unpack the food.

We worked without talking for a while.

There were patches of sunlight all over the floor, from the gaps between the boards. "When are you going to chink the walls, sir?" I asked at last, passing two jars of pickles down to where Mr. Thoreau stood in the cellar.

"In September, I would think. Till then, I will let the night breezes in. "

"My aunt says night air is bad for you."

He laughed. "So does mine. Do you suppose all of our aunts were cast from the same mold? Now, pass that jar of molasses, Will, and we'll be finished."

He climbed up, dropped the trap door into place and stood looking about him. "It is just as I hoped. What do you think, Will — do I lack for anything?"

The afternoon sun colored everything in the cabin a soft gold; it also showed up all the dirt we'd tracked in.

"Maybe a doormat," I answered.

"A lady did offer me one, but I prefer to wipe my feet on the sod before my door. Perhaps you'd take a broom to the floor, then come down to the cove. I will wait in the boat." He picked up his flute and went out.

I hadn't been alone in the cabin before. It was very quiet and peaceful. A good place to sit and think, for a while.

But a year seemed like an awfully long time.

And I remember reading how lonely Robinson Crusoe was.

As I stood there, a thin, sweet sound came from the pond, like a thrush's song.

Mr. Thoreau was playing his flute.

Chapter Four

He was sitting in his boat, facing the pond, his feet propped on a gunwale. Hearing Jessie bark, he laid down his flute and picked up the oars.

I pushed off, hopped into the stern and sat down. Jessie went on barking till we were out of sight, beyond the cove.

The sun had gone down behind the western pines; only the eastern shore was still in sunlight. The water was smooth as glass. Back by the cove, a loon called.

Concord seemed a hundred miles away.

Mr. Thoreau had stopped rowing. "This is my favorite time, this umbrageous hour," he said quietly.

"Does that mean shadowy, sir?" I asked, keeping my own voice low. "Or shady? Like under an umbrella?"

He reached over and clapped me softly on the shoulder. "Well done, Will! You have it exactly. Both are from the Latin word *umbra*, for shadow."

I felt like I'd gotten some sort of prize.

He rowed for a while, then rested on his oars, like he was listening for something.

"Sir?"

He seemed to come back from a long way off. "Yes, Will?"

"Aren't you afraid you'll be lonely here?"

"No more than a loon is lonely, or the pond itself."

I didn't say that I thought the loon's call was the lonesomest sound I knew.

"I do not fear solitude, Will," he went on. "I welcome it. I've built many castles in the air; now I need to put foundations under them. I've studying to do, and ideas I want to pursue, not all of them comforting to our fellow townspeople."

Like the squeaking pout, I thought. And the time he rang our church-bells to announce the anti-slavery meeting, when the sexton wouldn't do it. Father hadn't liked that; irresponsible, he'd called it.

"I want to write a book, too," Mr. Thoreau went on. "About the river trip that John and I made from Concord up into New Hampshire."

"In this boat?" I asked.

"No, that was the '*Musketaquid*,' named after our river. I sold her to Mr. Hawthorne and he re-named her '*Pond Lily*.' I prefer the Indian word."

Perhaps he wouldn't have time to be lonely, with his garden to tend, and his cabin to finish, and a book to write.

"And visitors," he said, like he'd read my mind, "when I was building my cabin hardly a day passed that someone didn't stop. I hope you'll come by sometime too, Will."

I was about to answer when the loon called again. This time we could see it, dark against the silvery water. I pointed; Mr. Thoreau nodded and began to row, quietly.

When we were about two rods off, the loon dove.

We waited till it rose again, nearer the shore. Mr. Thoreau seemed to know where it would come up, and each time it let us row a little closer.

Six times. Then it was gone. In the silence, a bull-frog gave its, 'Tr-r-oonk, tr-r-oonk .'

Mr. Thoreau chuckled and picked up the oars. "He always wins this game. We have played it nearly every evening the past two weeks."

A whippoorwill called and another answered, 'Poor-Will.' "I can set my watch by those two," said Mr. Thoreau. "And here comes my other time-piece. A noisy iron horse, but always prompt."

There was a rumble and a roar and then the early evening train from Boston rattled through the deep cut west of the pond.

Father and Ben would be coming out on the train, after the fireworks. It was time I got home.

"I would be happy to have you row," said Mr. Thoreau. So we switched places and I rowed us back, trying not to catch any crabs.

"Do you understand the meaning of the word 'deliberately,' Will?" he asked, gazing off across the pond.

"Yes, sir. It means on purpose. Robert said yesterday that I'd lost his best marble deliberately. I didn't, either. It just rolled into a knot hole."

"You have it. On purpose, or with purpose. That is how I want to live; with purpose. Consciously, aware of every moment. I cannot do so, living among society. Folk must be always asking me my plans for next week, next year. Today is my only concern."

I understood. I hated having Father's friends pat me on the head and ask what I wanted to be when I grew up. I hardly knew what I wanted to do the day after tomorrow.

We landed and hauled the boat above the water line. I'd kept an eye out for Jessie on the way in. Now I whistled and called, but she didn't come.

"I imagine we will meet her on our way back," said Mr. Thoreau as he untied the horses.

I hoped so. Jessie had never been so far from home.

"I will hunt for her tomorrow, if she has not returned," he said. "Now hop up, Will."

The team knew they were headed home. Once on the road, they settled into a steady trot. We passed a white dog walking alongside one of the Irishman who lived in town. He tipped his cap to Mr. Thoreau.

"Good evening, James Collins," said Mr. Thoreau, raising his hat in reply. "His former shanty provided the boards for my cabin. Four dollars and twenty-five cents I paid him. A fair price, do you think?" he asked, like he was talking to another man.

"Well, yes, sir. Seems so to me," I answered.

"Good. I would not want to have cheated James. The Irish worked hard on laying all those railroad tracks."

We were nearly in town when we heard it: a single drum, being played somewhere in the fields behind my house. Then I remembered that the Townsend Light Infantry often camped there on the Fourth. They usually went on to Boston, after our parade.

"Maybe he missed the train this morning," I said.

"Or perhaps he did not keep pace with his companions," said Mr. Thoreau. "Or the beat he heard was different. A different drummer..."

I don't know what else he was going to say, because just then we drew up in front of my house and Mother was standing on the porch with Jessie beside her, wriggling with happiness to see me.

"I was worried when she came home alone," Mother said, as we came up the path. "I hope Will was a help to you, Mr. Thoreau."

"Very much so, ma'am," he answered. "A hard worker. And the day was not without its pleasures, I think." He gave me a quick look, and his eyes were laughing.

Mother hesitated. "Mr. Crawford will be back on the next train," she said.

I knew what she meant. "Do I have to tell him where I've been?" Father would give me a talking-to, if nothing else.

"If he asks, yes, you must tell him," Mother said. "If not, well...we'll see."

"I do not reveal where the rarest wildflowers bloom, or where the fox dens," said Mr. Thoreau. "You will find me equally silent in this regard. And now I must return Mr. Hosmer's team. Good-night, Mrs. Crawford. Good-night, young Will, and thank you." He shook my hand, raised his hat to Mother, and strode quickly down the path.

I stood on the porch, fingering the arrowhead in my pocket, and watched till the team and Mr. Thoreau were out of sight.

I wished I was going with him.

Afterword

Henry David Thoreau was born in Concord, Massachusetts in 1817. After graduating from Harvard College, he taught for a while in Concord. All during his life, he was well respected in Concord as a surveyor, measuring the boundaries of people's properties with skill and accuracy, a perfect job for someone with his love of the out-of-doors. His keen observations of nature were noted in his careful journals and later published: *A Week on the Concord and Merrimack Rivers* came first, followed by *Walden*, which recorded what he saw and thought about during the two years and two months he spent in his cabin on the pond.

Over time, *Walden* has become one of the most famous books ever published in the United States, inspiring the environmental movement in this country and around the world. After Henry Thoreau died in 1862, his friends and family published his writings in *A Yankee in Canada, The Maine Woods, Cape Cod,* and other books.